## THE BOOKS ABOUT JOSEFINA

❋

### MEET JOSEFINA · An American Girl

Josefina and her sisters are struggling after Mamá's death, when a surprise gives Josefina hope—and a wonderful idea.

❋

### JOSEFINA LEARNS A LESSON · A School Story

Tía Dolores brings exciting changes for Josefina and her sisters. But will all the changes make them forget Mamá?

❋

### JOSEFINA'S SURPRISE · A Christmas Story

A very special Christmas celebration helps Josefina and her family heal their sadness.

❋

### HAPPY BIRTHDAY, JOSEFINA! · A Springtime Story

Josefina faces a terrifying adventure, and her birthday becomes a celebration of bravery—and second chances.

❋

### JOSEFINA SAVES THE DAY · A Summer Story

In Santa Fe, Josefina meets a surprising stranger—an *americano*. He's funny and friendly, but can he be trusted?

❋

### CHANGES FOR JOSEFINA · A Winter Story

Josefina is shocked when Tía Dolores announces that she's leaving the rancho. Can *anything* persuade her to stay?

*Also available in Spanish*

# CHANGES FOR
# JOSEFINA
*A Winter Story*

By Valerie Tripp

Illustrations Jean-Paul Tibbles

Vignettes Susan McAliley

Pleasant Company

Published by Pleasant Company Publications
© Copyright 1998 by Pleasant Company

Printed in the United States of America.
98 99 00 01 02 03 WCT 10 9 8 7 6 5 4 3 2 1

The American Girls Collection®, Josefina®, and Josefina Montoya®
are registered trademarks of Pleasant Company.

PICTURE CREDITS
The following individuals and organizations have generously given permission to
reprint illustrations contained in "Looking Back": pp. 60-61—*Chili Time, New Mexico,* by
Oscar E. Berninghaus, private collection; illustration from *Commerce of the Prairies* by Josiah Gregg
(wagon train); detail from painting by Carlos Nebel, ca. 1830 (two women); courtesy Museum
of New Mexico, Santa Fe, neg. #9927 (Cleofas Jaramillo); pp. 62-63—courtesy Museum of New
Mexico, neg. #9896 (Josiah Gregg); Center for Southwest Research, University of New Mexico
(book page*); Army of the West Entering Santa Fe, August 18, 1846,* by Don Spaulding. Courtesy
Don Spaulding and Sunwest Bank of Santa Fe; *Mexican War–Storming of the Heights,
April 18, 1847,* artist unknown, © Collection of The New-York Historical Society, neg. #36030;
pp. 64-65—*Through the Alkali,* by C.M. Russell. From the Collection of Gilcrease Museum, Tulsa,
neg. #0137.903 (cowboy); courtesy Nita Stewart Haley Memorial Library, Midland, TX (outlaws);
National Anthropological Archives, Smithsonian Institution, neg. #76-6644 (Apache women);
Ben Wittick, School of American Research Collections, Santa Fe, neg. #15780 (train);
Victor Higgins, courtesy Museum of New Mexico, neg. #40394 (painter); pp. 66-67—"The Next
Candidate for Statehood" from *Puck,* vol. L, no. 1294. Courtesy Minnesota Historical Society,
St. Paul. Reprinted in *Nuestras Mujeres: Hispanas of New Mexico, their images and their lives, 1582-
1992,* Tey Diana Rebolledo, editor; photo by Aaron B. Craycraft, courtesy Museum of New
Mexico, neg. #14145 (Santa Fe street); Jack Parsons Photography, Santa Fe (dancers).

Edited by Peg Ross and Judith Woodburn
Designed by Mark Macauley, Myland McRevey, Laura Moberly, and Jane S.Varda
Art Directed by Jane S.Varda

**Library of Congress Cataloging-in-Publication Data**

Tripp, Valerie, 1951-
Changes for Josefina : a winter story / by Valerie Tripp ;
illustrations Jean-Paul Tibbles ; vignettes Susan McAliley.

p.  cm.  —  (The American girls collection)
"Book six."
Summary: When Tía Dolores, the beloved aunt who has cared for the
Montoya family since the death of their mother, announces that she is planning
to leave, Josefina and her sisters try to find a way to change her mind.
ISBN 1-56247-592-4 (hc.).  —  ISBN 1-56247-591-6 (pbk.)
[1. Aunts—Fiction. 2. Sisters—Fiction. 3. Ranch life—New Mexico—Fiction.
4. Mexican Americans—Fiction. 5. New Mexico—History—To 1848—Fiction.]
I. Tibbles, Jean-Paul, ill. II. McAliley, Susan. III. Title. IV. Series.
PZ7.T7363Cgf  1998  [Fic]—dc21  98-24009  CIP  AC

TO ROSALINDA BARRERA, JUAN GARCÍA,
SANDRA JARAMILLO, SKIP KEITH MILLER,
FELIPE MIRABAL, TEY DIANA REBOLLEDO,
ORLANDO ROMERO, AND MARC SIMMONS
WITH THANKS

Josefina and her family speak
Spanish, so you'll see some
Spanish words in this book.
If you can't tell what a word
means from reading the story
or looking at the illustrations,
you can turn to the "Glossary
of Spanish Words" that begins
on page 68. It will tell you what
the word means and how to
pronounce it.

Remember that in Spanish,
"j" is pronounced like "h."
That means Josefina's name is
pronounced "ho-seh-FEE-nah."

# TABLE OF CONTENTS

JOSEFINA'S FAMILY

**PAPÁ**
*Josefina's father, who
guides his family
and his rancho with
quiet strength.*

**ANA**
*Josefina's oldest sister,
who is married and has
two little boys.*

**JOSEFINA**
*A ten-year-old girl
whose heart and hopes
are as big as the
New Mexico sky.*

**FRANCISCA**
*Josefina's sixteen-year-
old sister, who is
headstrong and
impatient.*

**CLARA**
*Josefina's practical,
sensible sister, who is
thirteen years old.*

TÍA DOLORES
*Josefina's aunt, who
lives with Josefina's
family on their rancho.*

ANTONIO
AND JUAN
*Ana's little boys,
who are three and
five years old.*

TÍA MAGDALENA
*Josefina's godmother,
a respected healer.*

ABUELITO
*Josefina's grandfather,
a trader who lives in
Santa Fe.*

ABUELITA
*Josefina's gracious,
dignified grandmother,
who values tradition.*

# GIFTS AND
# BLESSINGS

A whisper tickled Josefina's ear.
"Josefina," it said. "Wake up."

Josefina was as cozy as a bird in its
winter nest. But she pushed back her blanket and
opened her sleepy eyes. She saw her little nephews,
Juan and Antonio, crouched next to her. They were
so close that she could feel their warm breath on her
cheek and she could see, even in the darkness, that
their faces were bright with excitement.

"Look!" whispered Juan. He and Antonio held
up their shoes to show Josefina. "The three kings
were here! They put treats in our shoes!"

"Yours, too, Josefina!" said Antonio, with a
mouth full of sweets.

"Oh!" breathed Josefina. She sat up quickly and Antonio handed her one of her own shoes. In it, wrapped up in a scrap of clean cloth, there were pieces of candied fruits, slices of dried apples and apricots, and a small cone of sugar. Far down in the toe of her shoe there was a tiny goat carved out of wood that looked just like her pet, Sombrita.

It was early in the morning of January sixth, *La Fiesta de los Reyes Magos,* the Feast of the Three Kings. The night before, the children had followed an old tradition. They'd filled their shoes with hay and left them outside. The story was that the three kings would pass by on their way home from bringing gifts to the Christ Child in Bethlehem. The kings' camels would eat the hay, and the kings would leave sweets and gifts in the children's shoes to say thank you.

"The three kings were very generous to us," said Josefina as she nibbled a piece of candied melon.

Antonio sighed and Josefina saw that his shoe was already nearly empty. "My shoe's too small," he said, forgetting to speak softly.

"Shh!" shushed Juan. Josefina shared her

sleeping *sala* with two of her older sisters, Clara and Francisca. Everyone knew that Francisca was grouchy all day if awakened too early. "Antonio, you had lots of sweets," whispered Juan, who was five. "You ate them too fast!"

Antonio hung his head. Josefina felt sorry for him. After all, he was only three. This was the first year he'd put his shoe out. Josefina remembered very, very well how it felt to be the youngest and to have the smallest shoe and to be so excited that she ate up her sweets instead of saving them the way her older sisters did. All that had changed. Francisca and Clara considered themselves too grown up, so now Josefina was the oldest child in the family to put out her shoe. "You can have some of my sweets," she said to Antonio. "I need my shoe, anyway. I can't hop to the stream on one foot."

"*Gracias*," said Antonio. He popped one of Josefina's sweets in his mouth and hopped around the room, first on one foot and then on the other.

Josefina watched him as she neatly rolled up her sheepskin and blankets and propped her doll, Niña, on top. "You boys had better hop back to your room and get dressed," she said quietly. "There's lots to do to get ready for the *fiesta* tonight." There was always a big fiesta, or party, to celebrate the Feast of the Three Kings, which was the last day of the Christmas season.

Clara was awake by now. She opened the door and a blast of cold air as sharp as an icicle came through. Francisca groaned and pulled her blanket over her head. "It snowed in the night," Clara said. "If it starts again, there might not be any fiesta."

Antonio stopped hopping and Juan asked, "No fiesta?"

"Don't worry," said Josefina. Now that she was almost eleven, she didn't let Clara's unhappy predictions discourage her. "It's early yet. As soon as the sun comes up, the sky will be blue. I'm sure of it. Now go!" She shooed the boys back to the room they shared with their parents—Ana, Josefina's oldest sister, and her husband, Tomás. Then she pulled on an extra petticoat, warm socks, and her warmest *sarape* and headed to the stream.

Josefina fetched water for the household first thing every morning. She enjoyed going to the stream even on wintry days like this one because each day was different. Today fresh

*sarape*

4

new snow squeaked under her feet. The noisy stream greeted her, rushing around rocks capped with snow, then curving away out of sight. Josefina knew that the old saying *El agua es la vida* was true. Water was life to the *rancho*. Nothing could grow without it. The stream flowed along as steadily as time and blessed the rancho as it passed.

Josefina filled her water jar with the stinging-cold water. She put a ring of braided yucca leaves on her head and then balanced the jar on top of it. She walked back up the path thinking about all the delicious foods for the fiesta that this water would be used to make. There would be cookies called *bizcochitos*, spicy chile stew, and warm turnovers stuffed with fruit. Best of all, there would be dark, sweet hot chocolate. Josefina's feet moved faster at the thought of it.

Papá met her halfway up the path. "Oh, it's my Josefina," Papá said as he fell into step alongside her. "I thought you were a sparrow flying up the hill toward me. You're in a hurry this morning."

"*Sí*, Papá," said Josefina, "because of the fiesta tonight."

"Ah!" said Papá. "Tía Dolores tells me that you're going to play the piano at the fiesta. She says you have a gift for music."

Josefina blushed. "Tía Dolores is very kind," she said.

"Sí," agreed Papá. "She is." They walked a few steps and then he said, "I can remember when you'd have been much too shy to play music at a fiesta."

"I am worried about it," Josefina admitted. "I don't think I could do it at all if it weren't for Tía Dolores. She taught me the piece of music I'm going to play and we've practiced it a lot. It's a waltz. I'm hoping everyone will be so happy dancing that they won't notice my mistakes! I especially hope Tía Dolores will be dancing. No matter how flustered I get, if I can look up and see her dancing, I'll be fine. I'll pretend I'm playing only for her."

"I'll tell you what," said Papá. "I'll ask Tía Dolores to dance the waltz with me. Then you need not worry."

"Oh, will you, Papá?" asked Josefina.

"I promise," he answered.

When Josefina and Papá came to the house, they saw that everyone was up and beginning the

6

day's work. Juan and Antonio were energetically sweeping the snow out of the center courtyard. Or at least Josefina guessed that's what they were *supposed* to be doing. Actually, they were using their straw brooms to swoop the snow up into the air. Then they stood with their heads tilted back so that they could catch snowflakes on their tongues.

"I suppose we should stop them," said Papá with a grin.

Josefina didn't want to. The swirling snow was pretty. It glittered as it caught the early morning sun.

"Oh, please don't," said Tía Dolores, smiling as she came from the kitchen. She had a bundle of twigs, which she added to the fire already burning in the outdoor oven called the *horno*. "Ana has everything running smoothly in the kitchen. But we were tripping over those boys. They would not stop pestering us for tastes of food. They must have asked for cookies twenty times! Ana sent them out here, and the longer they're not in the way, the better."

*horno*

Papá laughed and Josefina's heart lifted, as it always did, to hear him. Josefina remembered how it was just after Mamá died. Back then Papá seldom laughed or smiled. She and her sisters had been crushed by sorrow, too.

Then, a little more than a year ago, Tía Dolores had come to stay with them. Josefina looked at her aunt laughing along with Papá and thought about the wonderful changes Tía Dolores had made. She'd taught Josefina and her sisters to read and write. She'd helped them weave blankets to sell and trade. She'd brought her piano to the rancho and taught Josefina to play. Many evenings Papá played his violin while Tía Dolores played her piano. The rancho was a different place because of Tía Dolores. Josefina thought the best change of all was that Tía Dolores had helped their family to be happy again— especially Papá.

"Come along, Josefina," Tía Dolores said now in her brisk way. "Ana needs that water in the kitchen."

"Sí," said Josefina, smiling to herself. One thing Tía Dolores had taught *everyone* on the rancho was her favorite saying: *The saints cry over lost time.*

No time was being lost in the kitchen! It was humming with activity. Ana, who was in charge, was making turnovers. Carmen, the cook, was stirring a big copper pot full of stew. Tía Dolores helped Carmen set the pot on an iron trivet over hot coals from the fire. Francisca's sleeves were rolled up and she was kneading bread dough.

"Bless you, Josefina," said Ana. She took the water jar. "Please help Francisca. I want the dough to rise while we're at morning prayers. The horno should be hot enough to bake the bread after prayers."

Clara was kneeling on the floor, using the *mano* and *metate*. She put a handful of dried corn on the flat metate stone and crushed it with the mano stone, rubbing back and forth until the corn was ground into coarse flour.

"Clara," Josefina said as she took off her sarape, "it's sunny. There's not one snow cloud in the sky."

Clara shrugged. "Not yet," she said, crushing another handful of corn. Then Clara surprised Josefina by smiling. "It's not that I want to be discouraging," she explained. "I just think it's foolish to get your hopes up the way you always do, Josefina. You're bound to be disappointed."

"I can't help it," said Josefina. "My hopes seem

to go up whether I want them to or not."

"Like this bread dough," joked Francisca. She pressed her fists into the dough and pushed down. "No matter how I flatten it, it rises up again."

"Hope is a blessing," said Tía Dolores.

"Sí," agreed Ana as she put some turnovers on a plate. "I think it's good to keep trying and never give up."

Just then, Juan and Antonio stuck their heads in the door. "Please," Juan asked for the twenty-first time, "can we have some cookies now?"

"What was that you said about never giving

up?" Josefina asked Ana. And suddenly the kitchen was full of laughter.

❋

After morning prayers and breakfast, Josefina and Tía Dolores carried the fat loaves of bread dough outside. Josefina took the wooden door off the horno, and smoke from the fire inside rose up into the blue sky. Josefina and Tía Dolores shoveled out the hot coals and swabbed the inside of the horno clean. When they finished, Tía Dolores put a tuft of sheep's wool on a wooden paddle.

"Oh, Tía Dolores, may I do it?" asked Josefina.

"Certainly," said Tía Dolores.

She gave Josefina the paddle, and Josefina put it into the horno. When the sheep's wool turned a toasty brown, Josefina knew the horno was just the right temperature to bake the bread.  Josefina used her finger to press the shape of a cross on the tops of the loaves as a reminder that all the earth's bounty was a gift from God. Then, as Tía Dolores watched, she carefully put the loaves into the horno and wedged shut the heavy wooden door.

"Well done!" said Tía Dolores.

*As Tía Dolores watched, Josefina carefully put the loaves into the horno.*

"I can take it out at the right time, too," said Josefina, boasting a bit.

"Good for you!" said Tía Dolores. "You don't need my help with the bread at all anymore, do you? But maybe I *can* help you practice the music you're playing tonight."

"Oh, yes, please," said Josefina. They walked together toward the *gran sala*, where the piano had been moved for the fiesta. "I'll practice playing the waltz, and perhaps you'd like to practice dancing it."

"Gracias," said Tía Dolores, laughing. "But that won't be necessary. I plan to be sitting right next to you at the piano while you play."

Josefina stopped and looked at her aunt. "Oh, but Tía Dolores," she said seriously. "Papá is hoping you'll dance the waltz with him. He told me so. You wouldn't want to disappoint him, would you?"

Tía Dolores slipped her arm around Josefina's shoulders. "No," she answered just as seriously. "I would never want to disappoint your papá."

Josefina was sure there had never been a more beautiful night for a fiesta. The huge, cold, black sky was sprinkled with stars, and the ground was silvery because of the moonlight shining on the snow. In the center courtyard of the house, a line of little fires lit the way to the gran sala, the biggest and grandest room, which was used only for special times like this.

Inside the gran sala, candlelight caught the bright colors of the ladies' best dresses and glinted off the men's buttons. Josefina and Clara were too young to dance, but they were allowed to sit on the floor and watch. Francisca swung by with her partner, and Ana waved gaily as she danced past with Tomás. Josefina saw stout Señora Sánchez and kindly Señora López both dancing with their husbands, and stately, white-haired Señor García dancing with his wife. The guests were friends from the village or from nearby ranchos, and Josefina had known them all her life. Somehow, though, their familiar faces looked different tonight. Perhaps it was the gentle glow of candlelight or just the magic of happiness that made the ladies look so lovely and the men look so handsome.

After a while, Clara nudged Josefina. "Time to

play your waltz," she said.

Josefina stood, smoothed her skirt, and straightened her hair ribbon.

"You look fine," Clara said. Then she stood too and said kindly, "I'll go with you. Come on." The two sisters walked through the crowded room to the piano. Josefina was pleased to see that Francisca and Ana were waiting for her there. They smiled encouragingly as she sat down.

Josefina had never played music in front of a large group of people before. Her hands were trembling. Then, out of the corner of her eye, she saw Papá bow and hold out his hand to Tía Dolores. Josefina began to play, and Papá and Tía Dolores began to dance. Josefina had always liked the lilting rhythm of the waltz, *one-two-three, one-two-three, one-two-three.* And tonight the music seemed to spiral up, up, up in ever more graceful swoops and swirls as she played. She never took her eyes off Papá and Tía Dolores. It was as if all the other dancers had faded away. Around and around and around Papá and Tía Dolores whirled. Tía Dolores danced so lightly in Papá's arms it seemed as if the music were wind and she and Papá were birds carried on it.

Around and around and around they danced. *Papá and Tía Dolores belong together,* thought Josefina. *They love one another.* With her whole heart, she was sure of it. Ana, Francisca, and Clara were watching Papá and Tía Dolores, too. Josefina knew that her sisters were thinking the same thought she was. And she knew they were wishing, just as she was, that the dance would never end.

16

# CHAPTER
## TWO
—
# SLEET

The bad weather Clara had predicted came howling in the next day. The sky was hard, dark and gray, and sleet clattered and bounced on the roof of the gran sala. Tía Dolores and the sisters had gathered in the gran sala to dust and sweep so that the room could be closed up until the next fiesta. The day was dreary, but Josefina needed only to close her eyes to imagine the way the gran sala had glowed with candlelight the night before. She hummed the waltz to herself as she swept.

Papá came in with two servants. They were going to move the table and chairs back to their usual places and put Tía Dolores's piano back in the family sala.

"Wasn't it a lovely fiesta?" Josefina sighed, looking at the piano.

"You know, I used to think a fiesta was hardly worthwhile," said Clara, sounding unusually cheery. "There's so much work to do to get ready and even more work afterward to clean up! But last night's fiesta was worth it."

"And just wait till you're old enough to dance," said Francisca, twirling around her broom. "Then you'll love fiestas as much as I do."

"Preparing for a fiesta used to overwhelm me," said Ana. "But Tía Dolores has taught me to enjoy it. Now I think it's a pleasure to cook food for our friends to share."

"You did a wonderful job," Tía Dolores said to Ana. "All of you did." She looked around at all the sisters. Josefina thought Tía Dolores's face looked pale, as if she had not slept well the night before. "I am proud of you."

Papá spoke up. "Tía Dolores is right," he said. "Thanks to your hard work, that was a fiesta we'll all remember with great pleasure."

"Gracias, Papá," said the sisters happily. Such praise from Papá and Tía Dolores was delightful indeed! They all went contentedly back to work.

Except for Tía Dolores. She asked, "Do you remember that when I first came here, I said I would stay as long as you needed me?" The sisters stopped sweeping and looked at her as she went on. "You've all learned to do your sewing and weaving and household tasks very well. And you all did so beautifully preparing for the fiesta yesterday! I can see that you don't need me the way that you used to. So . . . so I've written to my parents and asked them to come here and take me back to Santa Fe with them. I'm going home."

The room was completely silent. The sisters were stunned still. Josefina felt as if a drop of freezing sleet were running right down her spine. "But Tía Dolores, *this* is your home," she burst out. "We thought you were happy here with us!"

"I am," said Tía Dolores. Then she squared her shoulders and spoke firmly, as if she'd made up her mind after a long struggle with herself. "But it's time for me to leave."

Josefina turned to Papá. He looked as shocked as she felt. Surely he would say something to Tía Dolores! But Papá only bowed his head for a moment. When he looked up, his face was composed and grave. He left the room without saying a word.

Tía Dolores watched him go. Then she picked up her broom and went back to work. But Josefina and her sisters stared after Papá, as if he alone had the answer to a question that was desperately important to them all.

The more she thought about it, the angrier Josefina was with herself. Bragging about how she could make bread! Showing off playing the piano! *No wonder Tía Dolores doesn't feel needed!* Josefina thought. The sleet had stopped, but it was still very windy and cold as Josefina walked to the goat pen to see Sombrita. "But I know how to make things right," Josefina said to the little goat as it chewed on the fringe of her sarape. "I'll start tomorrow."

The odd thing was that her sisters seemed to have hit upon the same idea. The next morning, Francisca spilled tea at breakfast. Josefina was quite sure she did it on purpose. Francisca was wearing Clara's sash instead of her own, and the sash was badly stained. Francisca and Clara had sharp words about it, bickering just as they used to in the days before Tía Dolores had come and taught them to get along. Later that morning, Clara, who seldom made mistakes, snarled the wool, and four rows of weaving had to be disentangled from the loom. Ana somehow forgot to put salt in the sauce, so dinner tasted terrible. Josefina made mistakes all day long. She burned some *tortillas,* dropped a basket in a puddle, forgot part of a prayer, sat on her best hat, and was all thumbs at her piano lesson.

That evening Tía Dolores and the sisters gathered in front of the fire in the family sala. Papá didn't join them. His violin lay neglected on top of the piano. Last summer, Josefina and her sisters had traded blankets, which they'd woven themselves, to get that violin for Papá. It had belonged to an *americano* trader named Patrick O'Toole. *Papá might as well give the violin back,* thought Josefina with a sigh. *He'll have no pleasure in playing it if Tía Dolores leaves.*

No one had much to say. Then Clara dropped her ball of knitting yarn. She and Ana leaned forward at the same time to pick it up and knocked heads. Ana pulled back so quickly she jarred Francisca's elbow and Francisca pricked her finger with her sewing needle. Francisca yelped, which startled Josefina so that she made an ink splotch on her paper.

Tía Dolores shook her head. "I see what you girls are up to," she said. "You're deliberately bungling things so that it'll seem as if you still need me. But it won't work. And you'd better stop before one of you sets your skirts on fire!"

She laughed, and the sisters had to laugh at themselves, too.

"But Tía Dolores," said Clara, "we *do* need you." Sometimes Josefina was glad that Clara was so straightforward.

"Sí," agreed Francisca. "Not just as a teacher, but as part of our family."

"We were so unhappy and lost after Mamá died," said Ana softly. "And you made everything better."

"We need you because we love you," said Josefina.

"Bless you!" said Tía Dolores, not laughing anymore. "I love you, too. That will never change. But you girls have come a long way toward healing from the sorrow of your mamá's death, God rest her soul. Your papá has come a long way, too. It's time for him to marry again, to give his heart to someone. If I am here, I'm afraid I may be in the way. That's why it's time for me to go. That's why I *want* to go."

"Oh, but Tía Dolores!" said Josefina. "Papá—" But Ana squeezed Josefina's arm to stop her. They all knew it would be wrong for Josefina to finish her sentence and say to Tía Dolores, "Papá loves *you*." Children did not say such things to adults.

"Besides," said Tía Dolores with her usual briskness, "if I am going to start a whole new life for myself in Santa Fe, the sooner I begin, the better."

The sisters could not look at one another or at Tía Dolores. There was nothing more they could say to her.

There was, however, a great deal for Josefina, Francisca, and Clara to say to one another later when they were together in their sleeping sala.

"Maybe this cold, sleety weather will stop Tía Dolores's letter from getting to Santa Fe," said

Josefina, listening to the wind whistling outside the door. "Then Abuelita and Abuelito won't come to take her away."

"Don't be silly," said Clara. "Sooner or later, Tía Dolores is going to leave. Didn't you hear her say that she *wants* to go?"

Things were always black and white for Clara, plain as a wintry landscape of bare trees and snow. But Josefina saw glimpses of color even in the starkest view.

"I don't think it's that simple," Josefina said now. "I don't think Tía Dolores truly wants to leave. She loves us, and . . ." Josefina swallowed and went on boldly, "I think she loves Papá. He loves her, too, but she doesn't know it."

"That's right," said Francisca. She sighed dramatically. "How terrible to love someone and think he doesn't love you in return. No wonder Tía Dolores wants to leave. Her heart must ache every time she sees Papá."

"Heavens above!" groaned Clara. "What nonsense! Tía Dolores isn't so foolish."

Josefina spoke with great certainty. "I know that Tía Dolores would stay," she said, "if Papá—"

"Asked her to marry him," all three sisters finished together.

"Sí," said Josefina. "The truth is, I've hoped he would for a long time now."

"Well," said Clara calmly. "Papá and Tía Dolores would be a good, sensible match, and a practical one, too." All the girls knew it was not unusual for a man to marry his wife's sister after his wife died. The families already knew each other, and it kept their property together.

"If they do decide to marry, they shouldn't waste any more time about it," said Clara. "Neither one of them is getting any younger. Besides, it's always best to have a wedding in the winter so that it won't get in the way of planting or harvesting."

"Oh, Clara!" exclaimed Francisca. "How can you be so matter-of-fact? You're forgetting all the wonderful steps in courtship. First, Papá has to write a letter asking Abuelito for Tía Dolores's hand in marriage. Then Abuelito and Abuelita ask Tía Dolores if the proposal is acceptable to her. If it isn't, then to say no Tía Dolores must give Papá a squash—"

"There'll be no squash in this case. I'm sure of it!" Josefina cut in.

"And don't forget the engagement fiesta," Francisca rattled on, "and the groom's gifts to the bride, and—"

"Stop!" interrupted Clara. "There's one thing you're both forgetting: there's nothing *we* can do about *any* of this."

Josefina refused to give up. "There must be *something*," she said.

"Children are not involved in such matters," said Clara flatly. "It would be absolutely improper for us to talk to Tía Dolores or Papá."

Clara was right, as usual. But that did not stop Josefina. She thought for a while, and then she said, "I know someone we could talk to."

"Who?" asked her sisters.

"Tía Magdalena," said Josefina. Tía Magdalena was Papá's sister and oldest relative, and the most respected woman in the village because she was the healer, or *curandera*. She was also Josefina's godmother, and they had a special feeling for each other.

"When?" asked Clara.

"I'm sure Tía Magdalena will come to see

Abuelito and Abuelita while they're here," said
Josefina. "We'll ask her to speak to Papá. Oh, now
I'm *glad* Abuelito and Abuelita are coming! That will
make it all happen faster."

Francisca and Clara threw back their heads and
started laughing.

"What's so funny?" asked Josefina.

"You are!" said her sisters.

"You find the sweet in the sour," said Clara.
"The warm in the cold."

"The soft in the hard," added Francisca. "And
the light in the dark."

"Every time!" Clara and Francisca ended
together.

Josefina didn't mind her sisters' teasing. She
could tell that now they too were eager for Abuelito
and Abuelita to arrive.

They did not have to wait long. Abuelito and
Abuelita arrived from Santa Fe only a few days later.
And just as Josefina had expected, Tía Magdalena
came up from the village to see them the very first
afternoon.

Before, during, and after dinner, Josefina waited for a chance to speak to Tía Magdalena, but they were surrounded by family all the time. It was not polite for a child to draw an adult aside for private conversation. Josefina knew she'd just have to sit and watch and wait and listen and hope for a quiet moment. It was hard because she was bubbling over with secret excitement.

Juan and Antonio were excited, too. They loved to see their great-grandparents, Abuelito and Abuelita. The boys showed their happiness with their whole bodies, frisking and dancing about the family sala until Abuelita scooped up Antonio, held him on her lap, and sat Juan right beside her.

"These are the finest boys in New Mexico," Abuelita said to Ana. "I really think that they should be educated by the priests in Santa Fe. Juan is old enough, and Antonio will be soon."

"Sí," agreed Abuelito. "It's an exciting time we live in. It's important for the boys to be educated so they can keep up. The world changes so fast!"

"And not all the changes are good," said Abuelita. "So many americano traders are coming to New Mexico now, with their different manners and customs and language! Most of them don't even share our Catholic faith." She shook her head. "I fear our most precious beliefs will be lost if we don't do all we can to teach them to our children."

"Now, now," said Abuelito. "Not all the americanos are so bad." He turned to Papá. "Don't you agree?"

Papá nodded. "Señor Patrick O'Toole is an honest young man," he said. "I plan to continue trading mules and blankets to the americanos with his help. He's a good fellow. I look forward to seeing him soon when he passes by on his way home to Missouri."

Abuelito leaned forward. "Then you will be interested to hear my news," he said. "I've been invited to join Señor O'Toole's wagon train and travel with it to Missouri. And I've decided to go!"

Everyone gasped. Abuelito went on with a pleased expression on his face. "I'll travel with the wagon train over the Santa Fe Trail to Franklin, Missouri. Then I'll ride a steamboat to St. Louis! I'll bring goods to trade and

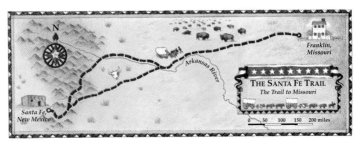

arrange for goods to be sent back here. What an adventure it will be! I guess I'm not such an old man after all!"

"May God watch over you," said Tía Magdalena, who'd been listening silently.

Josefina was trying to imagine what a steamboat might look like when Abuelito said something that made her heart stop.

Abuelito smiled at Tía Dolores. "You know, my dear, I must thank you," he said. "I wasn't going to accept the invitation. I didn't want to leave your mother alone all the months I'd be away. But when we got your letter saying that you wanted to come home, I knew I could say yes. Because you're coming home to Santa Fe, I can go to Missouri with the americanos!"

*Oh, no!* thought Josefina. *This is terrible.*

Then it got worse. "I was glad to get your letter, too, my daughter," said Abuelita to Tía Dolores. "Your father and I have waited a long time for you to come home to Santa Fe. It's such a comfort to know you'll be living with us as we grow old."

"I'm glad to be needed," said Tía Dolores softly.

*Needed!* Josefina felt a door slamming shut when

she heard the word. She and Francisca and Clara exchanged agonized looks. How could Papá ask Tía Dolores to marry him *now*? It would seem selfish, and it would hurt Abuelito and Abuelita. Tía Dolores would never say yes if Papá *did* ask her. Her first duty was to her parents. It would be unthinkable for her to let them down.

Josefina could not bear to hear any more. Quietly, she slipped out of the family sala, ran across the cold courtyard, and went to her sleeping sala. It was dusk, and the room was full of shadows. Josefina sat on the floor, hugging her knees to her chest.

She was all alone for a few minutes. Then someone came into the dark room and asked, "Josefina?"

It was Tía Magdalena.

Josefina jumped to her feet and stood, head bowed, in the respectful way children were supposed to stand in the presence of an adult.

Tía Magdalena sat on the *banco* and motioned Josefina to sit next to her. "All afternoon I've had the feeling that you wanted to ask me something," she said.

*banco*

"Sí, Tía Magdalena," said Josefina. "I did. But
. . . I beg your pardon, but I don't need to anymore."

"I see," said Tía Magdalena. But she didn't
leave. Instead she said, "I've invited your Tía Dolores
to stay with me for a few days before she goes to
Santa Fe with her parents. I've grown so fond of her,
and it'll be a long, long time before I see her again.
Santa Fe's too far for me to travel anymore. Ah, well,
we'll *all* miss your Tía Dolores very much when she
leaves, won't we?"

Now the words spilled out of Josefina. "Oh,
Tía Magdalena!" she said. "It will be terrible if
Tía Dolores leaves. It will be the way it was just
after Mamá died, when we were all so sad. We
were . . ."

Josefina faltered. Gently, Tía Magdalena finished
for her. "You were heartsick with sorrow," she said.

"Sí!" said Josefina. She spoke with conviction.
"Tía Dolores mustn't leave! She belongs here! I was
going to ask you to speak to Papá so that you could
ask him to . . . to set it all straight." Josefina shook
her head as she went on. "But now Abuelito and
Abuelita need Tía Dolores in Santa Fe. She *has* to
leave. There's nothing anyone can do."

32

*"Tía Dolores mustn't leave!" Josefina said. "She belongs here!"*

"Dear child!" said Tía Magdalena. "I'm afraid you're right. Curanderas don't have medicine for such troubles."

Josefina sighed. There was one narrow window in the sleeping sala, and only a sliver of the twilight sky showed through. Josefina could see just one star, a tiny pinprick of light, shining very far away. "With all my heart," she said softly, "I want Tía Dolores to stay."

Tía Magdalena took Josefina's hand in hers. "Here," she said. She put something as smooth and cool as a raindrop into Josefina's palm.

It was so dark, Josefina had to lift her hand close to her eyes to see what Tía Magdalena had given her. It was a *milagro*, a little medal. Josefina knew that a milagro was a symbol of a special hope or prayer. When someone wanted to ask a saint for help, he'd pin a milagro to that saint's statue. If he was praying to find a lost sheep, he would choose a milagro in the shape of a sheep. If he was praying for a hurt foot to heal, he would choose a milagro in the shape of a foot.

"I want you to keep this milagro with you," said Tía Magdalena. "It will remind you to pray for your family's happiness, for your sorrow to be healed. And perhaps it will help you not to lose hope in your heart's desire."

"Gracias, Tía Magdalena," said Josefina. She looked closer. The milagro Tía Magdalena had given her was in the shape of a heart.

# JOSEFINA'S PLAN

Early the next morning, Tía Dolores left Papá's rancho and went to Tía Magdalena's house in the village, which was about a mile away. It was a bleak day. The tree branches were coated with hard, new ice, and they clinked when the wind knocked them together.

All that day, Josefina thought that the rancho seemed to be under a terrible spell, frozen in gloom, even though everything ran smoothly enough. No one spilled tea or ruined weaving or burned tortillas. Dinner was well cooked and served on time. Josefina did not make one single mistake when she practiced playing the piano. And yet somehow, the music was all wrong. It was just noisy, clanging sound. There was no joy in it. Since the piano would soon be gone with Tía Dolores, there didn't seem to be much point in practicing anyway. There didn't seem to be much point in anything at all.

*This is what it will be like forever after Tía Dolores leaves,* thought Josefina sadly. She was wearing the heart milagro on a thread around her neck. Every time she moved, she felt the cool little heart touch her chest. She was grateful for its comfort. It was like a gentle voice saying, *Perhaps there's still hope. Perhaps there's a way Tía Dolores can stay. Perhaps tomorrow you'll think of something. . . .*

But the next day came and Josefina felt as dull as the weather. Fat gray clouds hung so low over the mountains that the snowy peaks poked through. Everyone seemed unhappy, except for Abuelita and Abuelito. Abuelito talked to Ana's husband, Tomás, about the new plow Tomás had bought from the americano traders and the new system of ditches Tomás and Papá had dug on the rancho to bring water to the fields.

*plow*

"That Tomás is a clever fellow," Abuelito said to

Abuelita. "He's not afraid of change. He did a fine
job managing the rancho last summer while the
rest of the family was in Santa Fe. I wish I had a
manager who'd do as well for me while I'm away."

Josefina and Abuelita were in the family sala
playing clapping games with Ana's and Tomás's boys,
Juan and Antonio. Abuelita looked at Abuelito and
smiled. "Cleverness runs in the family," she said.
"Ana manages this household as smoothly as any
I've ever seen. And I've never known two brighter
boys than little Juan and Antonio." She sighed and
hugged the boys. "Bless their dear hearts," she said.
"How I shall miss them when we leave! I wish I
could watch them grow and change!"

Josefina's brain seemed to wake up at that
moment. An idea started to take shape. She thought
about it all day, then presented her plan to Clara and
Francisca that night as they were getting ready for
bed. They sighed and shook their heads doubtfully
when they heard Josefina's idea.

But Josefina was determined. "We've got to *try*,"
she said.

So the next morning, Francisca, Clara, and
Josefina presented the plan to Ana. She spoke to

*Josefina and Abuelita were in the family sala playing
clapping games with Juan and Antonio.*

her husband, Tomás, and then all four sisters went together to Papá.

Papá was in the family sala. He had a pen in his hand and Tía Dolores's ledger book lying open in front of him, but he was staring into the fire when the girls came into the room.

The four sisters stood with their hands folded and their heads bowed, waiting for Papá to acknowledge them.

He turned and said, "Sí?"

"With your permission," said Ana, "we'd like to speak to you, Papá."

"Sí," Papá said again.

Ana looked at Josefina, Clara, and Francisca. They nodded to urge her to begin.

"Papá," said Ana respectfully. "Would you honor us by considering an idea we have?" She paused. "Do you think it might be possible for Tomás and our sons and me to go to Santa Fe with Abuelito and Abuelita?"

Papá looked at the fire again as Ana went on. "Tomás could manage Abuelito's rancho while Abuelito is away on his trip to Missouri," she said. "I could keep Abuelita company and help her run

her household. Juan could go to school and
be educated by the priests. And Antonio,
well, he will be happy to be with his dear
great-grandmother who loves him so."

*priest*

"Is this plan your idea?" Papá asked Ana.

"No," said Ana.

"It was Josefina's idea," said Clara.

Papá folded his arms across his chest and looked
at Josefina. Then he asked Ana, "Is this what you
and Tomás want?"

"Sí," answered Ana. "We'll be sad to leave here.
But this would be a step forward for Tomás and our
little family. I think it would be a good thing for
Abuelito and Abuelita, as well. It would be good for
you, too, Papá, and my sisters because—"

"Because then Tía Dolores would stay here!"
Josefina ended.

Papá's face softened. His voice was gentle when
he spoke. "I think this idea would be a wonderful
thing for almost everyone," he said. "But I'm afraid
that there is a problem with it. Tía Dolores has told
us that she wants to leave our rancho and go to
Santa Fe. If you go instead, Ana, she'll feel she's
needed here to help run our household. It seems to

me that all her life she's had to go where she was needed instead of where she wanted to go."

"But we don't believe that she really wants to go to Santa Fe," Josefina blurted out. "It's just that she thinks she should. You could convince her to stay, Papá!" Josefina didn't come right out and say *If you asked her to marry you,* but that is what she meant.

"Dear child!" said Papá, smiling. "You have a great deal of faith in my ability to change Tía Dolores's mind!"

"Please, Papá," asked Ana. "May we ask you to think about our idea, and perhaps consider presenting it to Abuelito and Abuelita? They may have an opinion about it."

"I will consider it," said Papá. "You have my word."

"Gracias, Papá," said the sisters. Quickly, they left the room.

"I don't think that went very well," said Clara.

"He *said* he'd think about Josefina's plan," said Ana.

"But he has to do more than that," said Francisca. "He has to ask Abuelito and Abuelita

for Tía Dolores's hand in marriage. She won't
stay here if he doesn't."

"Well, he'd better do it soon," said Clara.
"Tía Dolores will come back from Tía Magdalena's
any day now. As soon as she does, she'll leave
with Abuelita and Abuelito for Santa Fe."

"Oh, I hope Papá asks Tía Dolores to marry
him," said Francisca.

"He will!" said Josefina. "I just know Papá will!"

Josefina's sisters couldn't help but smile at her.

"Josefina," said Ana in her gentle way. "Don't
get your heart set on it."

"It's too late," Josefina said cheerfully. She
patted the heart milagro. "My heart's been set on
it for a long, long time already."

That very evening, when the family was
gathered in front of the fire, Francisca jabbed
Josefina to make her look up. Josefina tugged on
Clara's skirt and Clara nudged Ana. All four sisters
watched Papá hand Abuelito a folded piece of paper.
They heard Papá ask Abuelito, "Would you do me
the honor of reading this?"

"Of course!" said Abuelito. He and Papá and Abuelita left the room.

"Did you see that?" said Josefina joyfully. "Papá just gave Abuelito a letter asking for Tía Dolores's hand in marriage!"

"No, he didn't," said Clara. "The letter just presents the idea of Ana and Tomás and the boys going to Santa Fe."

Of course, there was no way of knowing who was right. But Josefina was sure she was, especially the next morning when she and Clara saw Abuelito and Abuelita setting out to walk to the village.

"Oh!" exclaimed Josefina, hugging Clara in her excitement. "Abuelita and Abuelito are going to ask Tía Dolores if she accepts Papá's marriage proposal!"

"No," said Clara. "They're just going to ask Tía Dolores how she feels about your plan. If she wants to go to Santa Fe, then Ana and Tomás won't go."

It was a blustery day and the whole sky was a pale, ghostly white, as if the clouds were full of snow waiting, waiting, waiting to fall. Josefina and her sisters were waiting, waiting, waiting, too, for Abuelita and Abuelito to come back from the village.

Josefina came up with a hundred excuses to go outside and look down the road to see if she could spot them returning.

"What could they be doing?" she fussed to her sisters. They were in the kitchen preparing the mid-day meal. A stick hung crossways in front of the hearth with dried squash and garlic and chiles dangling from it. Josefina tapped the stick to make the vegetables jiggle, as if they felt the same jittery impatience that she did. "Why is this taking so long? All Tía Dolores has to do is say yes or no!"

"*If* they're talking about marriage," said Clara, "which they're not."

Ana tried to soothe things. "Abuelito and Abuelita have many friends in the village," she said. "Their friends have probably come to Tía Magdalena's house to visit with them. And I suppose that Abuelito has told them that he's going to Missouri with the americanos, so they all have a lot to say. I'm sure everyone is surprised."

"Oh!" exploded Josefina. "In another minute I'll run to the village myself to see what is going on!"

"Heavens!" said Clara rather primly. "You can't

do that. Remember, this is none of our business. Children are not involved in such things."

Francisca rolled her eyes at Josefina and grinned. They knew that Clara was really every bit as curious as they were, though she liked to hide it.

It was late afternoon before Abuelito and Abuelita returned from the village, just in time for evening prayers. After prayers, as they all walked out into the courtyard, Abuelito turned to Papá.

"Well, Dolores surprised us," Abuelito said. The sisters were hardly breathing so that they could hear every word. "We discussed the idea of Ana and Tomás coming to Santa Fe instead of her."

Clara gave Josefina a look that said, "I told you so."

Josefina's heart sank. So Clara had been right. Papá's letter had *not* been a proposal of marriage. *Oh, Papá!* thought Josefina, bitterly disappointed.

Disappointment turned to horror and disbelief when Abuelito went on to say, "Dolores thinks that Francisca and Clara and Josefina are perfectly capable of running this household without her help *or* Ana's! She says it's time for her to leave even if Ana leaves too. She's coming to Santa Fe no matter

46

what Ana and Tomás do. So we'll pack up her belongings tomorrow, and we'll leave the day after."

"Very well," said Papá in a low, even voice.

*No!* Josefina wanted to shout out loud. *No!* Tía Dolores leaving *and* Ana leaving? That's not at all what was supposed to happen! Oh, how could her plan have turned out so badly? Hot tears filled Josefina's eyes. With a rough yank, she broke the thread with the heart milagro on it. She flung the milagro onto the slushy ground and walked away.

# HEART AND HOPE

When Mamá died, Josefina had thought that the world should stop.

It had seemed wrong to carry on with everyday chores, as if nothing had changed. But over time, she had learned that work was a great comfort in hard times. It was a blessing to do simple tasks like cooking and washing and sweeping, tasks that had to do with hands, not hearts.

Josefina felt that way the next morning. She was glad to go out into the biting cold to fetch water from the stream. She was glad the water jar was heavy and the hill was steep as she trudged back to the house. She was glad her heart pounded in her chest from the hard work, else she'd think it had withered from sadness. When Mamá died, Josefina had thought she could never feel that sad ever again. Now she knew she'd been wrong.

Papá met Josefina halfway up the hill, just as he had on the morning of the fiesta. But this morning, they walked in silence. They'd almost reached the house when Papá stopped. He reached into his pocket. "Josefina," he asked, "I found this in the courtyard last night. Is it yours?"

Josefina put her water jar on the ground and looked. She saw something muddy dangling from Papá's hand. It was the heart milagro. Josefina frowned. "It was mine," she said. "But I don't want it."

Papá held the milagro in his hand and wiped the mud off it with his finger. "I suppose there's nothing harder to give someone than a heart she doesn't want," he said slowly. "Tell me why you don't want this one."

"Tía Magdalena gave it to me," Josefina explained. "She said it would remind me to pray for our family's happiness, for our sorrow to be healed. And . . ." Josefina sighed, remembering. "She said it would help me not to lose hope in my heart's desire."

"I see," said Papá. The day's very first ray of sun peeked over the mountaintop and between two clouds. Papá tilted his hand so that, just for a second, sunlight found the milagro and made it shine. When he spoke, Josefina knew that he was trying to comfort her. "I know what your heart's desire was, Josefina," he said. "When you and your sisters came to me with your plan, I knew what you were thinking. You wanted to make it possible for me to ask Tía Dolores to stay here as my wife. That would have made you happy. And it would have made me happy, too."

Josefina looked at Papá with a question in her eyes. But he was looking up at the mountains, so he didn't see.

"The simple truth is that we can't always have what we hope for in life," Papá said. "Tía Dolores told us that she wants to leave, and so we mustn't stop her. When we love someone, *especially* when we love someone, we must let her go if she wants to go. We must put her heart's desire before our own." Papá turned to Josefina. "Do you understand?" he asked gently. "We want Tía Dolores to be happy, don't we?"

"Oh, but Papá!" said Josefina desperately. "Tía Dolores doesn't want to leave. She thinks she should, for *your* happiness. She said that it's time for you to give your heart to someone, and she's in the way." Then Josefina gathered up all her hope and courage and told the truth straight out. "Don't you see, Papá?" she said. "Tía Dolores loves you. That's why she *can't* stay. Because she thinks that you don't love her in return."

Papá shook his head and looked away from Josefina.

*It's no use,* thought Josefina. She lifted the water jar back onto her head and started to walk up the hill to the house.

"Josefina!" Papá called after her. "Do you want your milagro?"

Josefina turned. The heart milagro looked very, very small in Papá's hand. "No thank you, Papá," she said. "It's yours now."

Josefina did not see Papá again until the midday meal.

"Josefina," said Papá. "Your grandparents are

*"Don't you see, Papá?" Josefina said. "Tía Dolores loves you. That's why
she can't stay. Because she thinks that you don't love her in return."*

walking to the village this afternoon. They're going to bring Tía Dolores back here. I want you to go along to help."

"Sí, Papá," said Josefina, even though there was no walk in the world she dreaded more. She had no desire to help Tía Dolores begin to leave them!

Josefina, Abuelito, and Abuelita set forth for the village under a winter sun so pale it didn't warm the air at all. Josefina's nose hurt and her mouth had the bitter taste of cold in it. A mean wind made her eyes water, so she bent her head forward and pulled down the brim of her hat.

"Brrr!" shivered Abuelito. "That wind cuts through me! My hands are frozen stiff." He glanced at Josefina. "My child," he said. "Put this paper in your pouch and carry it for me." Abuelito handed Josefina a folded paper and she put it in a leather pouch that hung from a string around her neck. "Gracias," said Abuelito. He rubbed his hands together to warm them. "Oh, how glad I'll be to get to your Tía Magdalena's house and stand in front of her fire!"

They were *all* glad to come into the warmth of Tía Magdalena's house. A cheerful fire crackled on

the hearth, and steam rose in a cloud from a
big kettle. Tía Dolores smiled at Josefina, and
Tía Magdalena helped Abuelita sit next to the fire.
"Come! Sit and be comfortable," Tía Magdalena
said. "You must have a cup of tea."

"Gracias," said Abuelita. "You are very kind."

When they were settled, Abuelito said, "Josefina,
please give me the paper." Josefina took
the folded paper out of her pouch and
handed it to Abuelito. He gave it to
Tía Dolores, saying, "A letter for you,
my dear."

As Tía Dolores unfolded the letter,
something fell onto her lap. It was small and shiny
and bright as a spark in the firelight. "Why, what's
this?" asked Tía Dolores, holding the little object in
her fingertips and looking at it curiously.

Josefina gasped. *It was the heart milagro!*
Suddenly, Josefina knew. The letter was a proposal
from Papá! She was so happy, she wanted to jump
up and shout for joy. "It's a heart!" she exclaimed.
"It's Papá's! He's giving it to you. Oh, please read
the letter, Tía Dolores! Then you'll see."

Tía Dolores began to read the letter, and her

eyes grew wide. "Oh!" she exclaimed softly. Then, "Oh," she said again.

Everyone sat perfectly still, watching Tía Dolores. When she finished reading, Tía Dolores looked at Abuelito and Abuelita, and her face was lit with pure happiness. "Well," she said finally in a voice that trembled a little. "Josefina's papá has done me the honor of asking for my hand in marriage. Please tell him that my answer is yes."

"Bless you, my child!" exclaimed Abuelito. "We will."

Josefina jumped up and threw her arms around Tía Dolores's neck. She could feel Tía Dolores's happy tears on her own cheek.

On the day that Papá and Tía Dolores were to be married, the sun shone down on snow as white as new milk and dazzled the world with light. And yet the air carried a wisp of softness. Josefina took a deep breath as she walked up the hill from the stream. There was no mistaking the teasing hint of spring. She smiled to herself, thinking of the sprouts still sleeping under the snow, soon to

be awakened by the spring sun.

This morning, both Papá and Tía Dolores met Josefina partway up the path to the house from the stream. They stood together, smiling, as they waited for Josefina to draw near.

"Josefina," said Papá. "Tía Dolores and I want you to do something."

Tía Dolores pulled Josefina's hand toward her and put the heart milagro in it. "This is rightly yours," she said, "because you never forgot your heart's desire."

"Will you keep the heart milagro safe for us?"

asked Papá, smiling at Josefina with love.

"I will," said Josefina. "I promise."

Josefina remembered her promise later. She held the heart milagro in her hand as she stood outside the church after the wedding ceremony. Everyone she loved most dearly was gathered around her. Brave Abuelito, who was about to set forth on a new adventure. Dignified Abuelita, who held her chin up as if she were wearing a crown. Tía Magdalena, whose kindness and wisdom never failed her. Sweet Ana, her devoted Tomás, and their lively boys. Headstrong Francisca and sensible Clara. Josefina was sure that Mamá was there, too, in everyone's thoughts.

Villagers and neighbors, workers from the rancho, and friends from the *pueblo* cheered Papá and Tía Dolores, who smiled and waved. Musicians struck up a lively tune, and the church bell rang out joyously. A flock of birds, startled by the sound, rose up with a great exuberant fluttering of wings. Josefina smiled. She knew just how those birds felt. Her heart rose up with them into the endless blue sky.

# A PEEK INTO
# THE PAST

*A traditional home on a New Mexican rancho*

For more than 200 years, New Mexican settlers lived as the Montoyas did. But when Josefina was a girl, a time of great change was beginning for New Mexico.

The changes started in 1821, the year that Mexico won independence from Spain. Until then, foreigners—including people from the United States—were not allowed to do business in New Mexico. But after 1821, American traders began traveling to Santa Fe from Missouri. The wagon trail they took was called the Santa Fe Trail. Within just a few years, dozens of American wagon trains

*American traders arriving in Santa Fe*

were coming to Santa Fe every summer. Some New Mexicans, like Josefina's grandfather, also went to the United States to trade.

The flood of American goods began to affect the way New Mexicans dressed, did their chores, and decorated their homes. By the time Josefina was raising her own children, she might have had glass windows, wallpaper, and some American-style furniture, all brought to New Mexico by traders from the United States. By the time she was a grandmother, she might have given up comfortable, practical New Mexican–style clothes, like *rebozos*, full skirts, and loose blouses, and started to wear clothes that were fashionable in the United States, such as corsets, hoopskirts, and bonnets.

Even though Americans were happy to do business with New Mexicans, many of

*In the 1820s, women dressed in the comfortable, practical New Mexican style.*

*By the late 1800s, many New Mexican women—like the writer Cleofas Jaramillo, shown here—had adopted American fashions.*

*In 1844, an American trader named Josiah Gregg published a popular account of his travels in New Mexico. Books like Gregg's influenced how Americans thought of New Mexican life.*

them looked down on Mexican people or made fun of New Mexican customs they did not understand. They were shocked to see houses made of mud, and women wearing skirts that revealed their ankles! These travelers published reports in American newspapers and magazines criticizing many aspects of New Mexican life.

Still, people in the United States soon became interested in the Mexican lands to the southwest. They began to feel that these lands should belong to the United States. Many people believed that the United States was entitled to all of the land between the Atlantic and Pacific Oceans.

In December 1845, the United States government tried to buy Mexico's northern lands, including New Mexico. But Mexico refused to sell, and soon after, the United States declared war. American soldiers went to New Mexico on the Santa Fe Trail, and in

*American troops captured Santa Fe in August 1846.*

August 1846, they established American rule there without fighting any battles.

New Mexicans had very mixed feelings about the American takeover. Some were happy, believing that their chances for progress were greater if they were Americans. Others were angry and sad. When the American flag was first raised in Santa Fe, the women of the town wailed their grief so piercingly that even the cheering American soldiers were silenced. These women feared that their way of life and most precious New Mexican traditions would soon be lost.

The Mexican War was fought farther south and west until 1848. When the war ended, the United States had taken almost all the land that is now New Mexico, Arizona, California, Nevada, Utah, and Colorado, as well as

SANTA FE

In 1824, the purple area on the map belonged to Mexico. By 1848, all this land was part of the United States. The red line shows the U.S.-Mexico border today.

*American troops invading Mexico*

parts of other states. Everyone living in this region—except Native Americans—was granted American citizenship. Josefina would have become an American when she was 33 years old.

After the United States took over New Mexico, more and more Americans came from the East to do business or to settle. Protestant missionaries tried to convert New Mexicans from their Catholic faith. Cattle ranchers, miners, and outlaws made their way to New Mexico, too. During these years, many New Mexican families lost precious land or valuable rights to use water for irrigating their fields. In some cases, families had held their land or water rights for more than 200 years, but they had lost the papers to prove it. In other cases, American lawyers did not understand how Spanish and Mexican laws of ownership

*As New Mexico became part of the American West, cattle ranchers and cowboys moved into the territory. So did gun-slinging outlaws like the four men at left.*

worked. And some Americans simply took advantage of New Mexicans who did not speak English and tricked them out of their property.

Some of the Indian people of New Mexico experienced even greater changes. American soldiers fought long wars against the Apache and Navajo tribes and forced these people to live on lands set aside for them, called *reservations*.

*Young Apache women in the late 1800s*

In the 1880s, as railroads began bringing tourists and artists to the Southwest, Americans started to develop greater appreciation for New Mexico's landscape, climate, and cultures. Even so, Americans were not

*One of the first trains in New Mexico, in 1880*

willing to grant statehood to New Mexico for many years. One reason was prejudice against people of Spanish and Mexican heritage. Many

*Many famous artists were attracted by New Mexico's beauty. Their paintings encouraged other people to visit the Southwest.*

Americans thought that New Mexicans seemed too foreign to be "real" Americans. Finally, in 1912, New Mexico and Arizona were granted statehood—more than 60 years after the Mexican War ended.

*This political cartoon from 1901 shows New Mexico asking the U.S. for statehood. Many Americans did not want New Mexico to become a state because of its Spanish heritage.*

Like Josefina, many New Mexicans lived under three different governments—first Spanish, then Mexican, and finally American. Through all these political changes, life in New Mexico's small villages continued much as it had for generations. But in the larger towns and cities, changes were much greater. Many of the top government positions were held by Anglos, or English-speaking people from the East,

*American-style buildings and English street signs began to appear in New Mexico as more and more people from the eastern U.S. settled there. This photo shows a Santa Fe street in about 1905.*

not New Mexicans. Business and legal dealings were handled under United States law. Schoolchildren were taught in English.

New Mexicans—both Spanish and Indian—learned to take part in American life. But they also worked to hold on to their cultures—their faith, language, beliefs, arts, foods, and other traditions. Today the Southwest is a vital part of the United States that reflects all the cultures of the people for whom it is home—including Spanish, Mexican, Indian, and Anglo.

*A modern-day celebration of New Mexico's Spanish and Mexican heritage*

# Glossary of Spanish Words

**Abuelita** *(ah-bweh-LEE-tah)*—Grandma

**Abuelito** *(ah-bweh-LEE-toh)*—Grandpa

**americano** *(ah-meh-ree-KAH-no)*—a man from the United States

**banco** *(BAHN-ko)*—a bench built into the wall of a room

**bizcochito** *(bees-ko-CHEE-toh)*—a kind of sugar cookie flavored with anise

**curandera** *(koo-rahn-DEH-rah)*—a woman who knows how to make medicines from plants and is skilled at healing people

**El agua es la vida** *(el AH-wa es lah VEE-dah)*—a traditional New Mexican saying that means "Water is life." It shows how important water is to people living in a desert climate.

**fiesta** *(fee-ES-tah)*—a party or celebration

**gracias** *(GRAH-see-ahs)*—thank you

**gran sala** *(grahn SAH-lah)*—the biggest room in the house, used for parties and special occasions

**horno** *(OR-no)*—an outdoor oven made of *adobe,* or earth mixed with straw and water

**La Fiesta de los Reyes Magos** (*lah fee-ES-tah deh lohs REY-es MAH-gohs*)—the Feast of the Three Kings. This is the Catholic feast day that celebrates the Bible story of the three wise men bringing gifts to the baby Jesus.

**mano** (*MAH-no*)—a stone that is held in the hand and used to grind corn. Dried corn is put on a large flat stone called a *metate,* and then the mano is rubbed back and forth over the corn to break it down into flour.

**metate** (*meh-TAH-teh*)—a large flat stone used with a *mano* to grind corn

**milagro** (*mee-LAH-gro*)—a small medal that symbolizes a request that a person is praying for or a prayer that has been answered

**pueblo** (*PWEH-blo*)—a village of Pueblo Indians

**rancho** (*RAHN-cho*)—a farm or ranch where crops are grown and animals are raised

**rebozo** (*reh-BO-so*)—a long shawl worn by girls and women

**sala** (*SAH-lah*)—a large room in a house

**Santa Fe** (*SAHN-tah FEH*)—the capital city of New Mexico. The words mean "Holy Faith."

**sarape** (*sah-RAH-peh*)—a warm blanket that is wrapped around the shoulders or worn as a poncho

**Señor** (*seh-NYOR*)—Mr.

**Señora** (*seh-NYO-rah*)—Mrs.

**sí** (*SEE*)—yes

**tía** (*TEE-ah*)—aunt

**tortilla** (*tor-TEE-yah*)—a kind of flat, round bread made of corn or wheat

# THE AMERICAN GIRLS COLLECTION®

FELICITY    JOSEFINA    KIRSTEN    ADDY    SAMANTHA    MOLLY

Did you enjoy this book? There are lots more! Read the entire series of books in The American Girls Collection.® Share all the adventures of Felicity, Josefina, Kirsten, Addy, Samantha, and Molly!

And while books are the heart of The American Girls Collection, they are only the beginning. Our lovable dolls and their beautiful clothes and accessories make the stories in The American Girls Collection come alive.

To learn more, fill out this postcard and mail it to Pleasant Company, or call **1-800-845-0005**. We'll send you a catalogue full of books, dolls, dresses, and other delights for girls.

## I'm an American girl who loves to get mail. Please send me a catalogue of The American Girls Collection:

My name is _____

My address is _____

City_____ State _____ Zip_____

Parent's signature _____

## And send a catalogue to my friend:

My friend's name is _____

Address _____

City_____ State _____ Zip_____

If the postcard has already
been removed from this book
and you would like to receive
a Pleasant Company catalogue,
please send your name and
address to:

**PLEASANT COMPANY**
**PO BOX 620497**
**MIDDLETON WI  53562-9940**
**or, call our toll-free number**
**1-800-845-0005**